Usborne Farmyard Tales

WOOLLY STOPS THE TRAIN

Heather Amery
Illustrated by Stephen Cartwright

Edited by Jenny Tyler
Language Consultant: Betty Root

There is a little yellow duck to find on every page.

This is Apple Tree Farm.

This is Mrs. Boot, the farmer. She has two childre called Poppy and Sam, and a dog called Rusty.

his is Ted.

e drives the tractor and helps Mrs. Boot on the
rm. He waves and shouts to Mrs. Boot.

"What's the matter, Ted?" asks Mrs. Boot

"The train is in trouble. I think it's stuck. I can hea
it whistling and whistling," says Ted.

4

"We'll go and look."

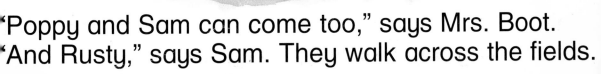

"Poppy and Sam can come too," says Mrs. Boot.
"And Rusty," says Sam. They walk across the fields.

5

Soon they come to the train track.

They can just see the old steam train. It has stopped but is still puffing and whistling.

"Look at those sheep."

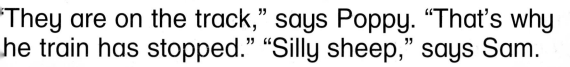
"They are on the track," says Poppy. "That's why the train has stopped." "Silly sheep," says Sam.

7

"It's that naughty Woolly."

"She's escaped from her field again," says Poppy.
"She wanted to see the steam train," says Sam.

"We must move them."

You can help me," says Mrs. Boot. "Come on, Rusty," says Sam. They walk up to the sheep.

9

"How can we get them home?"

"We can't get them up the bank," says Ted.
"We'll put them on the train," says Mrs. Boot.

"Come on, Woolly."

They drive the sheep down the track to the train.
Woolly runs away but Rusty chases her back.

"We'll lift them up."

"Please help me, Ted," says Mrs. Boot. Ted and
Mrs. Boot lift the sheep up into the carriage.

"All aboard!"

Poppy, Sam, Mrs. Boot, Ted and Rusty climb up
nto the carriage. Mrs. Boot waves to the driver.

The train puffs along.

It stops at the station. Mrs. Boot opens the door.
Poppy and Sam jump down onto the platform.

How many passengers?" says the guard.

Six sheep, one dog and four people," says Mrs.
Boot. "That's all."

"Let's all go home now," says Mrs. Boot.

They take the sheep back to the farm. "I think Woolly just wanted a ride on the train," says Sam.

First published in 1999 by Usborne Publishing Ltd., Usborne House, 83-85 Saffron Hill, London EC1N 8RT, England. www.usborne.com
Copyright © 1999 Usborne Publishing Ltd.